The
Patricia St John
Christmas Book

The Patricia St John Christmas Book

Illustrations by
Kaye Hodges

Scripture Union
130 City Road, London EC1V 2NJ

The stories in this book are taken from the following books
by Patricia St John:

A perfect Christmas from *The Tanglewoods' Secret*
The Christmas baby from *Treasures of the Snow*
Christmas in Morocco from *Star of Light*
The four Christmas candles from *The Secret of the Fourth Candle*

© Text: Patricia St John 1988
© Illustrations: Scripture Union 1988
First published 1988

Designed by Sue Ainley
ISBN 0 86201 532 4

Phototypeset by Wyvern Typesetting Ltd, Bristol

Printed by Ebenezer Baylis & Son Limited, The Trinity Press,
Worcester, and London

Contents

A letter from Patricia St John

This is a book about Christmas and we have taken these chapters from longer books because they show that all over the world, whether in snow or in bright sunshine, people come together to remember and rejoice over the gift of God's Son.

In a way, this is especially my book, because I took part in all these Christmasses. When I was a child my brothers and sister and I always pretended to be carol singers and my parents always pretended they didn't know it was us, and I shall never forget the brightness of the candles on the Christmas tree when it was already dark outside (no electric bulbs in those days). Then, when I was seven years old, we went to live in Switzerland and I can still feel the thrill and coldness of rushing down to church through the snow by moonlight on the big sledge, with my older brother holding me tight; and the delicious smell of those gingerbread bears. I never wanted to eat mine.

Much later, when I was grown up, I kept Christmas with the beggar boys up in the mountains and one of them brought me a starving kitten. This past year I went back to that little town and met some of those boys. Of course they are men now but they still remember the warm room and the charcoal fire and a few of them have not forgotten the stories of Jesus which they used to hear. I was also a nurse in the hospital on the cliff and I nursed many little 'Aishas'.

So when you keep Christmas, remember that many children all over the world will be hearing about Jesus for the very first time through some party or Christmas celebration. Perhaps you could spare a few minutes to pray that many of them will understand the greatness of God's love and the wonder of the Gift, and come back to hear more.

So I wish you all a very happy Christmas.

From your friend,

Patricia M. StJohn.

A perfect Christmas

*I*t was Christmas evening. We had had such a happy day that I kept having to stop and tell myself that it was all really true.

Mother and Father had arrived home from India just a fortnight before, and Philip and I had missed school and gone to Liverpool with Uncle Peter to meet the boat. We had been on a moving staircase, and we had stayed in an hotel where we had chicken and coffee-ices for supper, and we had gone up to bed in a lift and the lift man had let Philip work it. Then we had been wakened early, and gone down to the Merseyside in a wet, windy dawn; we had watched the passengers streaming down the gangway of the great liner, until Uncle Peter had suddenly said, in quite a quiet voice, 'Here they come,' and there were Mother and Father showing their passports at the barrier.

Philip, absolutely trustful and joyful, had flung himself straight into Father's arms, and had then turned to Mother and hugged the hat right off her head. But I stood still, because I wanted to be quite sure of everything first; and when Mother ran towards me I looked up into her face and suddenly knew that I had found something I'd been wanting all these years without knowing it. I was so overcome with this discovery that I just went on staring up at her, and she didn't hurry me. She waited, looking down at me, until I was ready and held up my arms to kiss her. Then she stooped and drew me to her, and there on the quayside, with the rain falling, and the crowds jostling, and the fog-horns wailing, she told me in a whisper how much she loved me, and I made up my mind, then and there, that I was never going to be parted from her again.

Then, with one hand in Mother's and one in Father's, and with Philip prancing round us like an excited puppy, we made our way back to the hotel, had kippers and toast and marmalade for breakfast, and nearly missed the train home.

And now it was Christmas evening and the great moment of the day was approaching. We had opened our stockings, and been to church, and eaten turkey and Christmas pudding until we all felt as tight as drums. We had been for a walk on the hills in the afternoon with Father and Uncle Peter, and had come back as hungry as though the dinner had all been a dream. We had had tea by rosy candlelight, Father had cut the cake with his Indian dagger and we had all pulled crackers, but little Minnie, one of the children from London who had come to spend Christmas in the country with us, didn't like the bangs and had been carried out screaming and fed with chocolate biscuits in the kitchen by Terry's mother. Now Auntie was saying, 'Run away for five minutes, children,' and Mother was saying, 'Go into the kitchen and see how Minnie is getting on,' and Father was saying, 'Anyone who comes into the drawing-room will be eaten by a big brown bear,' and Philip was pinching us all in turn and saying, 'Come on everybody, now's our chance.'

So when the drawing-room door was safely shut on the grown-ups, we slipped on our coats and tiptoed out of the front door. The world was quite silent and the starlight lay silver on the snow. Philip looked at us intently and hummed the note, and then we all threw back our heads and started singing:

> *The shepherds had an angel,*
> *The wise men had a star,*
> *But what have I, a little child,*
> *To guide me home from far,*
> *Where glad stars sing together*
> *And singing angels are?*

We sang the carol right through, and I kept on thinking that the Baby Jesus was now *my* Shepherd. The Shepherd who was going to look after me day and night and carry me home some day to where Terry was. I looked out into the wide white world with its snow, and smiled—I knew that I was perfectly safe for ever and ever.

But the carol was over and Alfie was hammering excitedly on the door. It was flung open, and there in the hall, under the mistletoe and holly, were Mother and Auntie in paper caps, and Father and Uncle pretending they didn't know it was us, and Terry's mother with tears in her eyes and little Minnie clasped tightly in her arms. We flung ourselves wildly upon them.

'Did you like it?' we shouted. 'Did you really think it wasn't us?'

But at that moment a piercing shriek from Lizzie made everybody jump. She had caught sight of something through the open drawing-room door and was making for it. With one accord we fled up the passage behind her and crowded in. The candles on the beautifully decked Christmas tree were alight and shedding a rosy glow over the dark room.

It was so pretty we stopped screaming, and sat down quietly, cross-legged on the floor, while Father started giving out the presents.

Soon it was our turn. Father took a square parcel from the pile at the bottom of the tree, and handed it to Philip.

'Open it carefully, Phil!' he warned. 'It's very fragile.'

Philip annoyed me by taking a long time over the unwrapping, but he always liked to spin out his pleasures as

long as possible. However, at last it came to light, and Philip made a funny noise in his throat like something trying not to explode. It was a black Kodak camera, just like the one we had so often gazed at in the chemist's shop.

'Philip!' I squealed, 'You've got it!' Then I stopped short, for of course it was my turn now. Father had selected a flat, hard parcel and was holding it out to me.

Everyone crowded round to watch as I, unlike Philip, tore the wrappings off as quickly as possible and gave a little gasp of delight and went pink all over.

It was my own picture of the Good Shepherd, but not a crumpled, torn postcard one. It was a big, beautiful copy in a carved wooden frame for me to hang over my bed and keep for ever. In fact, it was just like the one in Mr Robinson's study.

The grown-ups opened their presents after that, and seemed as pleased as we were; they were mostly home-made things and we were very proud of them: fret-work book ends for Uncle Peter, a purse for Aunt Margaret, a blotter for Father and a hot-water cover for Mother; Terry's mother was presented with a highly-coloured embroidered hanky sachet, which she admired very much indeed.

Of course there were other presents, too, but these were the main ones.

Philip and I helped clear up, and then Philip and Father sat down on the sofa and looked at the bird book together for about the tenth time. But it was different now, because the camera lay in Philip's lap and they were planning the photos.

I wandered off by myself with my picture in my arms, and climbed the stairs. I wanted to curl up behind the curtain on the landing window-sill and look at the Christmas stars and snow, and listen to the bells that were ringing from the church nearby. But when I reached my hiding place, I found that Mother had got there first, and that was even better than being alone, so I climbed on to her lap and held up my picture because I wanted us to look at it together.

'Isn't it beautiful?' I asked.

'Yes,' replied my mother, 'but what made you love it so specially, Ruth? Tell me about it.'

So I told her rather shyly, about the Shepherd who had found me, and she listened, looking out over the snow, until I had finished.

'And it's not only me,' I ended up; 'He found me first but after that he found Philip and Terry's mother, and he found Terry, too, and carried him right home; and, Mummy, sometimes I think perhaps he found Aunt Margaret, too. At least, I think she had forgotten about him a bit, and when she saw the picture it reminded her of him again.'

'Yes, I think it did,' answered Mother, 'and do you know, Ruth, I also want to learn so much more about him; won't it be lovely all learning together? Sometimes, far away in India, I used to kneel down and pray that somehow you would get to know about him, but I never felt I knew enough to teach you myself.'

I looked up quickly.

'Did you really?' I exclaimed. 'Then I suppose that's why it all happened. I suppose you sort of sent him to us. I'm glad it's like that, because it makes it even nicer than it was before.'

I laid my head against her shoulder, and we sat quite quietly looking out. I think I nearly fell asleep, and in a half-dreaming way I saw us all sought and found, and following through the green fields in Terry's picture: Mother and Father, Auntie and Uncle; Mr and Mrs Robinson and the twins, their tiny feet stumbling through the daisies; old Mr Tandy with his flock behind him; Terry's mother; Philip and me; Alfie and Lizzie and Minnie – because I had promised to tell them all about my picture in the morning; and in front of us all, the Good Shepherd with the wounded hands leading us on to a Land far away, where Terry, perfectly strong and happy, was waiting for us to come.

The Christmas baby

*I*t was Christmas Eve, and three figures were climbing a steep white mountain-side in Switzerland, the moonlight casting shadows behind them across the snow. The middle one was a woman in long voluminous petticoats and a dark cloak over her shoulders. Clinging to her hand was a black-haired boy of six, who talked all the time with his mouth full. Walking apart, with her eyes turned to the stars was a little girl of seven. Her hands were folded across her chest, and close against her heart she carried a golden gingerbread bear with eyes of white icing.

The little boy had also possessed a gingerbread bear, but he had eaten it all except the back legs. He looked at the little girl maliciously. 'Mine was bigger than yours,' he announced.

The girl seemed unconcerned. 'I would not change,' she replied calmly, without turning her head. Then she looked down again with eyes full of love at the beautiful creature in her arms. How solid he looked, how delicious he smelt, and how brightly he gleamed in the starlight. She would never eat him, never! Eighty little village children had been given

14

gingerbread bears, but hers had surely been by far the most beautiful.

Yes, she would keep him for ever in memory of tonight, and whenever she looked at him she would remember Christmas Eve—the frosty blue sky, the warm glow of the lighted church, the tree decked with the silver stars, the carols, the crib, and the sweet sad story of Christmas. It made her want to cry when she thought about the inn where there was no room. She would have opened her door wide and welcomed them in.

Lucien, the boy, was annoyed by her silence. 'Let me taste yours, Annette; you have not begun it.'

But Annette shook her head and held her bear a little closer. 'I am never going to eat him,' she replied; 'I am going to keep him for ever and ever.'

They had come to a parting of the ways. The crumbly white path lined with the sledge-tracks divided. A few hundred yards along the right fork stood a group of chalets with lights shining in their windows and dark barns massed behind them. Annette was nearly home.

Madame Morel hesitated. 'Are you all right to run home alone, Annette?' she asked doubtfully, 'or shall we take you to the door?'

'Oh, I would much rather go alone,' answered Annette, 'and thank you for taking me. Good night, Madame; good night, Lucien.'

She turned and fled, lest Madame should change her mind and insist on seeing her to the door, when she so badly wanted to be alone.

She wanted to get away from Lucien's chatter and wrap herself round with the silence of the night. How could she think, and look at the stars, when she was having to make polite replies to Madame Morel and Lucien?

She had never been out alone at night, before, and even this was a sort of accident. She was to have gone to the church on the sleigh with Father and Mother; they had all been thinking about it and planning it for weeks. But that

morning her mother had been taken ill and her father had gone off on the midday train to fetch the doctor from the town up the valley. The doctor had arrived about teatime, but he could not cure her in time to get up and go to church as Annette had hoped he would, so to her great disappointment she had had to go instead with Madame Morel from the chalet up the hill. But when she had reached the church it had been so beautiful that she had forgotten everything but the tree and the magic of Christmas, so it had not mattered so much after all.

The magic lingered; and now, as she stood alone among snow and stars it seemed a pity to go in just yet and break the spell. She hesitated as she reached the steps leading up to the balcony, and looked round. Just opposite loomed the cow-shed; Annette could hear the beasts moving and munching from the manger. A glorious idea struck her. She made up her mind in a moment, darted across the sleigh-tracks and lifted the latch of the door. The dear warm smell of cattle and milk and hay greeted her as she slipped inside; she wriggled between the legs of the chestnut cow and wormed her way into the hayrack. The chestnut cow was having supper, but Annette merely flung her arms around her neck and let her go on munching, for even so surely had the cows munched when Mary sat among them with her newborn Baby in her arms.

She looked down at the manger, and to her excited fancy it seemed as though the heavenly Babe were lying in the straw, with the cows, still and reverent, worshipping about him. Through a hole in the roof she could see one bright star, and she remembered how a star had shone over Bethlehem and guided the wise men to the house where Jesus lay. She could imagine them padding up the valley on their lurching camels. And surely shepherds would come stealing in with little lambs in their arms and offer to cover the Child with woolly fleeces. As she leaned further over a great wave of pity swept over her for the homeless Babe, against whom all doors had been shut.

'There would have been plenty of room in our chalet,' she whispered, 'and yet perhaps after all this is the nicest place. The hay is sweet and clean and Louise's breath is warm and pleasant. Maybe God chose the best cradle for his Baby after all.'

She might have stayed there dreaming all night had it not been for the gleam of a lantern through the half-open door of the shed, and the sound of firm, crunchy footsteps in the snow. Then she heard her father call her in a hurried, anxious voice.

She slipped down from the rack, dodged Louise's tail, and ran out to him with wide open arms.

'I went in to wish the cows a happy Christmas,' she said, laughing. 'Did you come out to find me?'

'Yes, I did,' he replied, but he was not laughing. His face was pale and grave in the moonlight, and he took her hand and almost dragged her up the steps. 'You should have come in at once when your mother is so ill. She has been asking for you this last half-hour.'

Annette's heart smote her dreadfully, for somehow the Christmas tree had driven everything else out of her mind, and all the time her mother, whom she loved so much, was lying ill and wanting her. She had thought the doctor would have made her well. She drew her hand from her father's and ran, conscience-stricken, up the wooden stairs and slipped into her mother's bedroom.

Neither the doctor nor the village nurse saw her until she had crept up to the bed, for she was a small, slim child who moved noiselessly as a shadow. But her mother saw her, and half held out her arms. Annette, without a word, ran into them and hid her face on her mother's shoulder. She began to cry quietly, for her mother's face was almost as white as the pillow and it frightened her. Besides, she felt sorry for having been away so long.

'Annette,' whispered her mother, 'stop crying; I have a present for you.'

Annette stopped at once. A present? Of course, it was Christmas. She had quite forgotten. Her mother always gave her a present, but she usually had it on New Year's Day. Wherever could it be? She looked round expectantly.

Her mother turned to the nurse. 'Give it to her,' she whispered. And the nurse drew back the blanket and produced a bundle wrapped in a white shawl. She came round to Annette and held it out to her.

'Your little brother,' she explained. 'Let us go down by the fire and you shall rock his cradle. We must leave your mother to sleep. Kiss her good-night.'

'Your little brother,' echoed her mother's weak voice. 'He is yours, Annette. Bring him up and love him and look after him for me. I give him to you.'

Her voice trailed away and she closed her eyes. Annette, too dazed to speak, allowed herself to be led downstairs by the nurse. She sat down on a stool by the stove to rock the wooden cradle where her Christmas present lay smothered

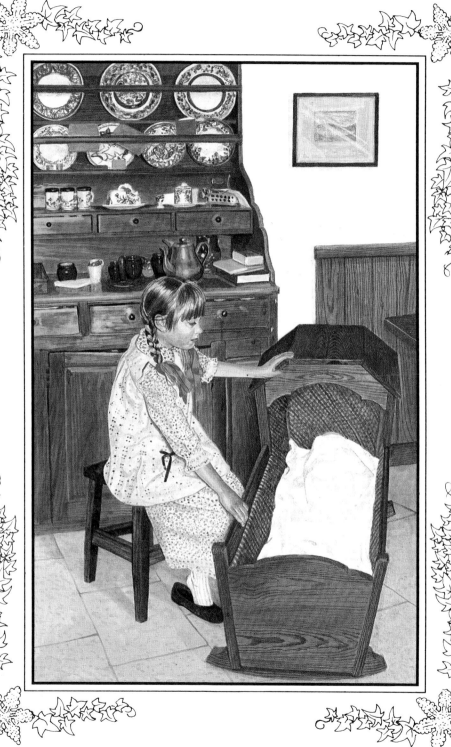

in shawls and blankets.

She sat very still for a long time staring at the hump that was her little brother. The snow cast a strange light on the walls, and the glow of the stove burned rosy on the ceiling. The house was very, very still, and the Christmas star shone in through the unshuttered windows. So had it shone on that other Christmas Baby in the stable at Bethelehem, and so had Mary sat and watched God's little Son, just as she was sitting by the stove watching her little brother.

She put out reverent fingers and touched the top of his downy head, which was all she could see of him. Then with a tired sigh she leaned her head against the cradle and let her fancy roam where it would—stars, shepherds, little new babies, shut doors, wise men and gingerbread bears—they all became muddled up in her mind, and she slid gradually on to the floor.

And it was here that her father found her an hour later, lying as peacefully asleep as baby brother, her bright head pillowed on the cradle rocker.

'Poor little motherless creatures,' he said as he stooped to pick her up; 'how shall I ever bring them up without her?'

For Annette's mother had gone to spend Christmas with the angels.

Christmas in Morocco

*H*amid and Ayashi crept shivering from the mosque one morning to find the olive groves and mountains above the town white with snow. The winter season had come to stay.

One week was particularly cold and bleak, and on a night of drizzling rain the children arrived at the door as usual and knocked impatiently, for the wind seemed to be cutting them in two, and their sodden, fluttering rags clung to their bodies. The door was opened at once, and they tumbled over the threshold, eager to reach the warmth of the fireside. But once inside the passage they stood arrested and staring, the cold and the rain forgotten.

For instead of the bright glare of electric light, they found themselves facing the soft blaze of candles set circlewise on a little table in the middle of the room, with silver boughs of olive wreathed round them. On the floor, arranged like a picnic on a coloured cloth, a feast was spread. There were nuts, almonds, raisins, sweets, oranges, bananas, sugar biscuits and honey cakes, and on a tray in the corner a shining teapot and a collection of little glasses. A kettle sang merrily on the glowing charcoal, and the room seemed warm and welcome. Even Kinza had stayed up to the feast. She sat on a cushion, holding a big red-and-white rubber ball, her face lifted expectantly.

'It's the Feast of the Christians today,' explained the nurse to the wide-eyed little boys, 'so I thought we would keep it together. It is the Feast of the birth of Jesus Christ. He was the greatest gift God ever gave, so at his Feast we all give presents to each other. That is why Kinza has a rubber ball, and that is why I've bought you sweets and oranges and bananas.'

The children sat down to their feast, a little awed at first by the strangeness of the silver light and their own pleasure; but gradually their tongues loosened, their toes and fingers thawed, and their cheeks flushed. They talked and ate merrily, tucking away their fruit and sweets in their rags to eat later, and sipping glass after glass of sweet, hot mint tea.

Hamid could not take his eyes off Kinza. She was dressed in her very best blue smocked frock and her curls were brushed out like an aureole. How round and sturdy she had grown! He suddenly remembered the white-faced, ragged little sister of past winters, the mud in the village, and the poverty and wretchedness. All that seemed shut out now: they seemed to be sitting cut off from the bleak world outside, in a warm, kind circle of candlelight. The children were talking about feasts in general, and he began to talk too. He began telling them about the sheep feast in his own village, and the nurse, watching his eager face, felt glad. He too had changed lately. He had never told her what had happened to him the night he took the eggs, but his manner was so different these days. He was no longer a shy, hesitating little stranger; he took his place confidently and expectantly every night, and his whole being seemed to respond to the story of the Saviour's love. So she sat watching him, longing to know what had taken place in that child-heart; until her attention was suddenly caught by a little drama going on at her side.

Kinza had risen to her feet, and there was a look on her

face the nurse had never seen before. It was a look of dawning, half-perceived memory, as though she had heard some dearly-loved but forgotten sound. Then, groping a little uncertainly, feeling her way with touch and hearing almost as sensitive as sight, she moved towards the speaker, and stood beside him, irresolute, tense.

At any other time Hamid would have been frightened at his secret being discovered, and would probably have pushed Kinza away. But there was an atmosphere in the room that night that cast out fear and suspicion, and Hamid, forgetful of everyone else, put his arm round his little blind sister, and drew her to him, while she, not knowing who he was, but somehow stirred and drawn by the voice she had once loved, nestled up to him, and laid her shining head comfortably against his wet rags. And the nurse, watching in amazement, suddenly noticed how astonishingly alike they were. A number of little incidents that had seemed unimportant up to now, flashed into her mind: the almost simultaneous appearance of the two children from nowhere; Hamid's strange request to see Kinza asleep, and the secretive way he had watched her in the street. She suddenly felt quite sure that they were brother and sister; but, even if she were right, it was of no practical importance. Hamid was unlikely to betray his secret, and she on her side had no intention of parting with Kinza. She could only guess what sad misfortune had cast these two little wanderers adrift into the world, and marvel at the loving-kindness that had led them to the haven of her own home.

The other children stared too. 'She knows his voice,' they said wonderingly, and they too glanced at each other with surprise. But they would not speak their thoughts in front of the nurse, and soon forgot about it in further glasses of mint tea. Then, the feast being ended, the nurse made them turn round and look at a white sheet hung on the wall. She blew out the guttering candles, and pictures appeared in the dark. The boys thought it was magic, and watched wide-eyed and open-mouthed.

It started with a picture of a man and a woman knocking at the door of an inn, but they had to go away because there was no room. Hamid felt sorry for them, because he, too, on his first night in town, had stood and gazed into the inn, longing for shelter. He had had no money, so he had slept on the rubbish heap, but the woman had gone into a stable, and the next picture showed them installed among the oxen. But a wonderful thing had happened. She had brought forth her first-born Son, and swaddled him, just as his own mother had swaddled Kinza, and laid him in a manger. Kinza had had a wooden cradle, he remembered, but this Baby was the child of very poor people, no doubt—homeless outcasts like himself.

But what was the nurse saying? The Baby in the manger was the Lord Jesus Christ, in honour of whose birth all Christians kept the feast of giving. He was God's great gift, and he had come willingly. The stable in the picture looked rather dark, lit only by one small lantern, but the home of the Son of God in Heaven was bright with the light of glory and love. Why had he left it?

The nurse was just telling them: 'Though he was rich, yet for your sakes he became poor.' He left the light and came into the dark, a homeless, outcast Child, in order to lead homeless, outcast children to the shelter and love of his Father, God.

And now there was a third picture: there were shepherds on the hillside keeping watch over their flocks by night; and Hamid thought of his own goats, and the days he had spent with them on the mountain—but here was another picture: the Angel of the Lord appeared, and the glory of the Lord shone round about them. They were afraid; but apparently the sheep were not. They seemed to be grazing quietly in the bright shelter of the Angel's wing. 'Unto you is born a Saviour,' said the Angel to the assembled company, and even the open heavens and the singing hosts failed to alarm the flock. Hamid suddenly remembered the anguished cries of the sheep dragged to their slaughter on the first day of the sheep feast. But here was no crying and no slaughter. There was peace in Heaven and goodwill on earth.

Then the last picture was flashed on the screen. The shepherds had left their flock to the care of the Angel, and here they were, barefoot, in their rough fleece coats, kneeling and worshipping at the manger. Hamid again thought of the sheep feast; the rich and the great of their land gorging themselves with fine food, and flinging what was over to the beggars and the dogs. But this was their very own feast. It was Kinza's feast, because Jesus had become a little Child, wrapped in swaddling clothes and it was his feast because the King of Heaven had become homeless and had been laid, outcast, among the cattle.

It was over. The nurse switched on the lights, and the picture faded. There was nothing visible left of the feast but gutted candles, sweet-papers, orange-peel and banana-skins. But the thought of a love that gave, and of a love that became poor, lingered with Hamid as he stepped out thoughtfully into the wet street. Kinza stood in the doorway,

waving to the sound of their retreating footsteps, and as he passed he put out a shy hand and touched her hair.

The other boys had gone on ahead, but Hamid loitered along slowly, the pictures still bright in his head, unconscious of the drizzling rain. As he passed under a blurred street-lamp a sharp little mewing caught his ears, and he looked down and saw a skeleton-like kitten, very small and wet, trying to shelter behind a drain-pipe.

In his eleven years of life he had seen many starving kittens dying in the street, and had never given them two seconds' thought. But tonight it was somehow different. He could not possibly have explained, but he had just been drawn close to a Child who was lowly and gentle and compassionate, and all unknown to him the first seeds of gentleness had been sown in his heart. He found to his surprise that he cared about the starving little creature, and he picked it up and held it against him. It was so thin that its skin seemed to be stretched tightly over its bones, and he could feel its rapidly thumping heart.

What should he do with it? He had no doubts at all. There was one open door where it would certainly be welcome, and Kinza would probably love it. It would be his Christmas gift to her.

He pattered back over the wet cobbles and knocked at the nurse's door. When she opened it, he held out the shivering, wretched creature with perfect confidence.

'It is for Kinza,' he explained, 'a gift of the feast. It is very hungry and cold, so I brought it to you.'

The nurse hesitated. The last thing she really wanted just then was a half-dead ginger kitten, covered with sores and vermin, but she could not refuse, because of what lay behind the gift. With a thrill of joy she realized that her evening's work had not been in vain. One little boy at least had understood, and entered into the spirit of Christmas. He had wanted to give, and he had been gentle and kind to an outcast kitten. It was the first time in all her experience that she had seen a Moorish child care about the sufferings of an animal.

So she accepted it gratefully and joyfully, and then holding it at arm's length she carried it to a box near the fire and sprinkled it all over with a disinfectant powder. Then she gave it a saucer of milk, and it twitched its tail at an impertinent angle, and lapped it up—a tough, gallant little kitten, unconquered by adversity! It deserved to be saved.

As she sat watching it she had a sudden vision, which passed swiftly and left her laughing. She thought she saw all the Christmas love-gifts of all the ages heaped together before the manger—the gold, the frankincense, the myrrh, the stars, the homage of heaven, the treasure and worship of earth. And perched on top of the glittering pile, precious in the eyes of the One to whom it was given, was a thin, flea-ridden, ginger kitten, with its tail at an impertinent angle—the first-fruits of a little boy's compassion.

The four Christmas candles

The Third Candle

Sunday was drawing to a close and the Boulevard was a blaze of light and festivity. Only one more Sunday before Christmas, and the great shop windows were wonderfully bright. And at sunset that evening Petra and her mother had lit the third Advent candle.

'And,' said Petra, 'when I light the fourth it will be time to hang up my stocking!'

Her mother laughed and kissed her and told her to run along because on Sunday night Petra's mother usually went to a party and she was in a hurry to be off. Petra nestled longingly against her and clung to her for a moment. She loved the feel of her mother's cool satin dress, the softness of her fur cape and the sweet smell of her cheeks. If only her mother was not quite so pretty and admired she would not have to go to quite so many parties! Then she would have time to come up to the nursery and stand in the beautiful white circle of the three Christmas candles and whisper lovely Christmas secrets. Now the car was at the door and her mother was off and away down the passage with a delicious rustle of flouncy skirts. Petra gave a little sigh and climbed the staircase alone, her evergreen wreath in her hand.

But she did not really mind about her mother tonight, because tonight undoubtedly the funny little girl would come, and Zohra would talk to her in her own language and tell her all about the candles, and she would show her the Christmas presents all wrapped up in holly-paper, put away in a private drawer. She laid her precious light on the table and went in search of Zohra and the coal bucket.

'Zohra,' said Petra in her most wheedling tones, 'I want you to stay with me tonight. I have a secret and you must help me.'

Zohra had no idea what a secret was, but she was always ready to help her adored Petra, so she smiled indulgently, laid down her bucket of coals, and sat down by the fire to wait and see what might be required of her. One never knew with Petra. She sometimes did have the strangest ideas.

'There is a little girl coming to see me,' explained Petra importantly, 'and she only speaks your language. I want you to tell her what I tell you and I want to show her my Christmas presents.'

This sounded innocent enough. Zohra smiled enthusiastically and nodded; probably, she thought, this was a little school friend, the daughter of some rich Moor, whose mother was bringing her to call.

But just at that moment there was a tiny rustle and movement, and the smile died on Zohra's countenance and gave place to a look of extreme indignation. For round the door there appeared a tousled head wrapped up in an extremely dirty cloth, and a pair of bright anxious eyes set in a smutty little face. The bright eyes did not see Zohra at first. They gazed enraptured at the three candles burning on the table, and the lips parted.

'There she is!' cried Petra joyfully, and she rushed to the door, dragged her disreputable companion into the room,

and slammed it behind her. 'I *knew* you'd come,' she said to Aisha. 'Look, I've lit the third candle!'

Aisha could not understand a word but she was delighted at the warmth of the child's welcome, and for a moment her face glowed with love and joy. Then it suddenly turned blank with fear for she had caught sight of Zohra in the shadows and Zohra's face was anything but welcoming. Aisha turned and made a dash for the door but Petra stood in the way and grabbed hold of her firmly.

'You are not to run away!' she said imperiously. 'I am going to tell you all about my candles. Zohra, you are to tell everything I say to this little girl, so she can understand it, in Arabic.'

Zohra shook her head helplessly. She recognized Aisha – the grimy child who scrubbed the scullery on Sundays. How the impertinent little creature had ever got into the nursery was more than she could understand, and she was quite sure Petra's mother would be very angry.

'Your mother wouldn't like it,' said Zohra in her broken speech. 'You know she wouldn't.'

'My mother's gone to a party,' retorted Petra impatiently. 'Don't be silly, Zohra. Do what I tell you. This little girl is my friend. Tell her that I light one candle every week on Sunday night for the coming of the Baby Jesus. Tell her that next week is the feast of his coming. Tell her to be sure to come back next week and see, because on Sunday I shall light all four candles and hang up my stocking and then it will be Christmas.'

Zohra sighed, but decided that the best way to get rid of this unwelcome little visitor was to do what Petra wanted. So she repeated the first two sentences in Arabic like a parrot, but allowed herself a little poetic licence with the rest. 'She says,' explained Zohra, 'that she lights one candle every week for the coming of the Baby Jesus and next week is the feast of his coming and she will light them all – but what you think you are doing here I don't know, you naughty little thing, and don't let me ever catch you in this nursery again or I'll hand you straight over to Fatima in the kitchen.'

Aisha gazed at her sorrowfully and doubtfully. The three candles were burning just as she had known they would be burning, but somehow it was all spoiled. The white circle of light was no longer a welcoming sanctuary of purity and gentleness; there was someone who didn't want her and she felt afraid and wanted to run away.

But perhaps it didn't matter, because the little girl most certainly did want her and the little girl was, after all, queen of the nursery. Now she suddenly took Aisha's hand and drew her to a corner of the nursery and opened a drawer full of parcels done up in holly-paper and golden string.

'Tell her they are my presents, Zohra,' commanded Petra, 'presents for everyone in the house and all my uncles and aunts. And tell her that if she'll come again next Sunday I will make a present for her.'

'She says they are her presents,' interpreted Zohra, 'and now for mercy's sake do get back to the kitchen and don't come up here again, there's a good child!'

She did not speak unkindly, for Aisha was a child of her own race, and probably meant no harm, but she was frightened of being scolded if such a very sooty, greasy creature were found in Petra's nursery. If only she could get rid of her now, she would speak to Fatima about it before next Sunday. Fatima would certainly prevent such a thing ever happening again.

Aisha looked awestruck at the candles, and then back at the presents, and almost forgot Zohra. She knew at last why the little girl lit one more candle every week. It was in honour of a Baby called Jesus who was coming next week, and then all the candles would burn and the whole room would be white and radiant and the Baby would laugh and crow. She had never heard of Jesus before, for she was a Moslem girl, but she felt sure he must be a very important Baby to have the candles lit specially for his coming. And all those presents, too! She supposed they were all for him and she wondered what was inside them – lovely little garments perhaps, and toys and tiny coloured shoes. She wanted to see him more than she had ever wanted to see anything else in the world. If only that woman would stop looking at her so disapprovingly and spoiling it all. She suddenly became conscious of Zohra again, and shyness and fear overcame her. She gave one quick grateful smile at the little girl, bolted for the front door and made off down the stairs as swiftly and silently as she had come. But before she reached the bottom again the clear urgent voice of Petra called after her.

'Venga – Domingo otro.'

Aisha's mother was in a hurry to get back home that night but she had hard work in getting her daughter up the Boulevard. Aisha seemed lost in a dream, dawdling, pressing her nose against every shop window until her mother slapped her.

She did not mind much. There were such lovely things in the shops and although she hadn't a single peseta of her own she wanted them all for the Baby. That tiny pink rabbit-wool coat for instance. He would look sweet in that; and that bright stick of sugar-candy – surely he would enjoy that! Already she loved him passionately with all the love of her newly-awakened little heart, and one great idea was slowly possessing her. She would give him a present, too. Next Sunday she would steal upstairs into the room where the four candles would be burning. She would not stay – just see him for an instant, kiss his chubby hand and lay her present at his darling feet with the curly baby toes, and then slip back into the dark, satisfied.

The question was, what present could she take him?

The Gift

She thought of little else all that week. It rained nearly every day, the cold, torrential winter rain of North Africa, and the children crouched round a clay pot of burning charcoal and tried to warm their stiff fingers and toes. The goats and hens came into the house for shelter and were very much in the way and under foot. The roof leaked, the baby coughed and wailed and snuffled, and everybody got on everybody else's nerves. It was a most trying week for everyone – except for Aisha, who nearly drove her mother crazy by her dreamy absent-mindedness and the stupid new habit she had acquired of sitting gazing into the charcoal, apparently quite unconscious of all the turmoil around her.

She saw wonderful pictures in the charcoal; pictures of herself kneeling, glorified by the candle-light, her hands piled with glittering gifts at the feet of a Baby who crowed and stretched out his arms towards her and who seemed in some mysterious way to radiate love and joy. Sometimes, when she was asleep at night cuddled under a sheepskin with Safea, the Baby came right into her arms and she felt, in her dreams, the warmth of his sturdy little body pressed against her and knew that if she could only hold him fast she would never be lonely or afraid again. Then she would wake to the coldness of the grey morning, with the drip of the rain through the thatch, and to the bitter realization of empty arms and empty hands – for after all, what could she take him?

Nothing – she had nothing at all! Gradually the truth forced itself upon her and she stood depressed in the doorway gazing at the spoiled mimosa tree, when her mother seized her by the shoulder and gave her a good shake. 'You do nothing all day but stand and stare,' shouted her outraged mother. 'You are no more use in the house than a cow – and the baby has spilled the grain under your very nose! Now go to the well and bring me two buckets of water quickly and don't stand all the afternoon staring into the water.'

She gave her a final push through the doorway and out into the grey rain. Aisha sighed and picked up her buckets and set off shivering. It was horrible going to the well this weather, but there was no help for it. She ran as fast as she could, clatter, clatter down the hill, but she couldn't run back. The hill was very steep and the buckets very heavy and the merciless rain half-blinded her; and worst of all she had no present for the Baby. She was miserable!

Walking with her head well down she bumped straight into old black Msouda who was also going to the well, grumbling, mumbling, moaning and shivering. Black Msouda lived in the hut next to Aisha and it was very hard on her having to draw water at her age, but the orphan grandson who lived with her had broken his arm and there was no one else to do it. She was very angry with Aisha for pushing into her and Aisha was just about to be rude back when she noticed that the old woman was crying: hopeless little sobs of weariness and cold and weakness came from under the towel that covered her bowed head.

Silver candle-light and a smiling Babe who radiated warmth and gentleness and love – an old woman slipping in the mud, weeping with weariness and cold. Aisha suddenly felt terribly sorry for her. She set her buckets down in a safe place by the side of the path and took Msouda's buckets out of her hands.

'I'll fetch your water, Msouda,' she said. 'You go back home.' She turned back down the path leaving the old woman gaping with astonishment. When she returned, Msouda had gone into her hut and was busy looking for something under the trestle that served for a bed.

Aisha set down the buckets in the doorway with a clatter and turned to go, but Msouda suddenly came out from under the bed and ran after her and thrust something soft and sticky into her hand.

'You are a good girl,' she said, 'and I'll give you one of my newly baked khaif.'

Aisha stood quite still in the rain, staring at her treasure,

her heart suddenly flooded with joy and sunshine, because these is nothing babies like better than khaif. It is a sort of flat concoction of flour and water, sprinkled in oil and baked on a flat pan. Babies eat it in greasy little pawfuls, and get very oily and happy in the process.

She was so excited that she ran home as far as the bamboo fence without her buckets, and then suddenly remembered and had to go back for them. Fortunately her mother had not seen her. She walked back into the house as though nothing had happened, and nobody knew about the wonderful secret she was hugging inside her.

She had no pretty paper like Petra but she chose a couple of flat shiny leaves and hid her khaif between them and placed it in a safe corner under the sheepskin. At night she took it to bed with her. It does not matter if you lie on top of a khaif because it is flat in any case.

Conveying it to town next day without her mother seeing

was difficult, as Aisha's clothes were of the scantiest. She laid it on top of her head and put the towel over it and walked with extreme caution and dignity. By the time she reached the big house she had a stiff neck and was glad to wrap the khaif up in her towel and lay it in the corner of the kitchen. Then somehow she must live through the long hours of the day until the lights began to twinkle in the streets and she could run up the magic staircase and see the four candles burning and lay her gift at the feet of the Baby.

She kept wondering if the Baby had arrived yet and once or twice she tiptoed to the passage and listened furtively for the sound of happy cooing or contented chuckling. But all was quiet and the door where the little girl lived was tight shut, so it did not trouble her much. Perhaps the Baby was coming by ship and they had all gone down to the port to meet him. The sun shone in wintry gleams on the water, breaking through the clouds and showing glimpses of the coast of Spain across the Straits, and Europeans smiled gaily and said that it would be fine for Christmas after all.

Twilight – the crowded Boulevards a blaze of colour and light – because all the shops were open on Christmas Eve, Sunday or no Sunday. Aisha's mother was busy as usual in the yard and Fatima had disappeared. Aisha was all alone in the kitchen and the moment had obviously arrived to go and look for the Baby. Even now they would surely be lighting the fourth candle. Hope, love, fear, courage, awe and longing, all flooded her simple little heart like a great tide, and drove her breathless into the dark passage, clasping the precious khaif tightly against her chest.

She tiptoed to the bottom of the staircase and looked up. The door was once more ajar and the soft welcoming light streamed towards her – a little stronger and clearer than before because tomorrow would be Christmas and Petra had lit all four Advent candles in honour of the Festival.

It was very quiet. Perhaps the Baby was asleep. Aisha, rosy with joy, scuttled up the staircase towards her fairy-land.

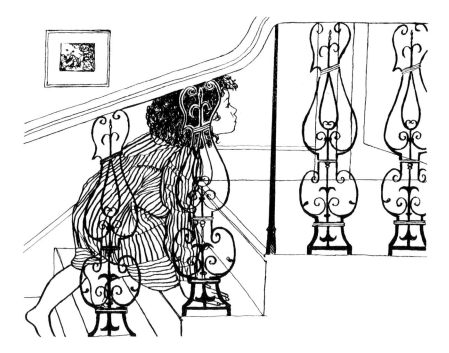

But as she reached the top of the stairs a rough hand shot out and seized her by the arm, and too bewildered to cry out she found she was being hustled downstairs; slapped and shaken, stumbling and gasping, she was at the bottom before she was really aware of what had happened, and then the light from the kitchen shone on Fatima's furious face so terrifyingly near her own.

'Yes, I know all about it,' snarled Fatima, who dared not make too much noise in the passage. 'Zohra told me – sneaking upstairs right into my lady's room; I thought I'd just catch you at it tonight – you try that again – this is the end of you – I'll tell your mother of you.' – Slap! slap!

Aisha, coming to her senses, gave a loud scream. Fatima clasped her hand over her mouth, pushed her through the front door and slammed it behind her. She was alone on the steps, still clasping her khaif to her heart.

She had no idea where she was going, but she must get

away somehow from the terrible Fatima, and she started running down the gay Boulevards, bumping into the people, noticing nothing, sobbing bitterly. But it was not the slapping or shaking that she really minded – in fact she hardly thought about them at all. What really mattered was, she had not seen the Baby. She had crept within a few yards of him; without a doubt he had been there, fast asleep in a soft cradle, lapped in the light of four candles, but the khaif that was to have been laid reverently on his quilt was still in her hand.

She was so lost in grief that she never heard the people shout or the policeman blow his whistle or the scream of brakes as she dashed blindly across the road. Nor could she ever remember afterwards being knocked over by the big car. She lay unconscious in the road and the crowds gathered round her, all chattering in different languages, until the ambulance arrived and drove her to the English hospital on the cliff overlooking the Straits of Gibraltar.

The Baby

She did not wake properly till twilight the next day because she had struck her head on the kerb and concussed herself slightly; also her leg had been broken by the wheel of the car. She half woke during the afternoon, and thought she heard the sound of singing very far away and thought she saw candles burning: but it might all have been a dream.

But when she woke at dusk she knew quite well she was not dreaming. She was wide awake and her leg hurt her and she felt giddy, but where she was she could not imagine. After a while she gave up trying to imagine and just lay quite still, looking and listening.

She was lying on a raised bedstead, which was slightly alarming because she had never slept anywhere but on the floor. However, there was a whole row of other people on raised bedsteads and they did not appear to be falling out so perhaps it was quite safe after all. At the other end of the room there were groups of people all looking at a tree, and among the evergreen branches burned, nor four candles, but many, many candles all different colours; under the boughs stood a row of children in long, bright silk dresses, singing in Arabic –

Away in a manger, no crib for his bed,
The little Lord Jesus laid down his sweet head.

Aisha's heart gave a sudden leap. 'The little Lord Jesus' – that was the name of the Baby who was going to stay with Petra, but apparently he was here instead, for they were singing about him and had lit at least fifty candles in honour of his coming. All other events were still confused and blurred, but Petra, the Baby, and the four candles were all perfectly clear in her mind.

She fell asleep again and when she woke it was night and there were no candles – only one tiny red lamp glowing above the door, casting a dim light over the room. Nor was there any more singing – only the snoring of sleeping patients.

Aisha lifted her head cautiously from her pillow and looked round. The night nurse noticed her and came over to see how she was feeling.

Aisha liked nurses. Just a year ago the youngest baby but one had accidentally sat down in the clay bowl of red-hot charcoal and Aisha had carried him to this same hospital every morning for his dressings. The nurse had always been kind and pleased to see her and once she had checked Absalom's yells with a pink sweet. Nurses were definitely friendly and trustworthy. Aisha smiled and kissed this one's hand by way of greeting.

'I want to see the Baby!' said Aisha. 'Where is he? Has he gone to sleep yet?'

'Which baby?' asked the nurse gently. 'Do you mean your baby brother?'

'No, I don't,' answered Aisha, 'I mean the Baby called Jesus. He was going to Petra's house and then he came here instead. The children sang about him and all the candles were lit. Where is he? . . . I had a present for him but I don't know where it is now.'

The nurse was puzzled. How had this little Moslem child with her big anxious black eyes heard of the Blessed Babe? And who was Petra? She sat down on Aisha's bed and tried to explain.

'Aisha,' she said, 'you cannot see the Baby Jesus because he was born many years ago and now he has gone back to God. But the children were keeping the Feast of his birthday and singing how he came into the world to save us from sin and sadness. I'll tell you about him, Aisha, and then you'll understand.'

Aisha lay very still, her black eyes fixed on the nurse's face. She wanted to understand about the Baby more than anything else in the world.

'God loved us, Aisha,' said the nurse, 'so he sent his Son the Lord Jesus to show us the way to Heaven. He became a little boy like us. His mother was very poor and laid him in a manger when he was born. He has gone back to God now, but he is still alive and he still loves us. He is with us all the time although we can't see him and he can still show us the way to Heaven.'

She shook up the child's pillow and moved away noiselessly, and Aisha lay staring at the red glow of the tiny lamp, thinking, thinking.

She had imagined herself running into the love-light of that candle glow for one moment, flinging her gift at the feet of the Baby, and then running back into the cold dark for ever. Now it was all different. He was not coming after all, and she would never see him; yet she was not unhappy, for the nurse had told her something even better.

'He loves you. He is with you all the time although you can't see him. . . . He will show you the way to Heaven.' That was what the nurse had said, and half-asleep and half-awake she fancied she saw a long bright road winding away through the darkness. At the beginning of the road stood the Baby, beautiful and rosy, tousled and bright-eyed as though newly awakened from sleep. In one hand he clasped a lighted candle and with the other he beckoned to her to follow him, and the love of his happy heart drew her irresistibly just as the glow of light had drawn her up the dark stairway. In her dream she ran to him and put her hand into his and knew that she had found everything she had ever wanted in her life and that nothing need ever frighten her or hurt her again, because no one could take the Baby from her or her from the Baby. And in the presence of the Baby there was safety and love and shelter and fulness of joy.

When All the Candles Were Lit

Aisha's leg was broken quite badly and she stayed in hospital six weeks and enjoyed every moment of it. But the highlights of the day were at three o'clock in the afternoon when her mother came to visit her, with the baby tied on her back and all the little brothers and sisters trailing behind, and seven o'clock at night when the English missionary appeared with a portable harmonium and they all sang hymns and heard wonderful stories about what happened to the Baby when he grew up.

She loved hearing how he laid his hands on sick people and made them better without any medicine at all, and on little children and sent them away happy and good and blessed, and on a dead little girl about Aisha's age who had sat up at once and felt hungry. But one night the English missionary told a very sad story of how those kind hands had been nailed to a cross of wood, and the Lord Jesus had been put to death. He had died willingly and lovingly to pay for all the wrong things that Aisha and everyone else in the world had done, and this made Aisha very sorry for she knew that she had very, very often told lies and lost her temper and been rude to her mother and slapped the babies. She lay thinking about it far into the night and once again she half dreamed, half imagined that the Baby came and held out his little hands to her and this time she could see that they had been wounded; and she knew that all the wrong things she had done could be forgiven and she could start all over again, with a heart washed clean and white.

'All my life I am going to follow the Baby in the path that leads to God,' she whispered, clasping her small hands. She loved him with all her heart and longed to give him a gift. She thought of beautiful little Petra lighting candles for his coming and wrapping up presents. She wished she too could light candles – but she couldn't. She was just a poor, common child with nothing to give.

After a time she was presented with some crutches and

allowed to leap around the garden, then she was allowed to walk alone with a stick – and one beautiful spring day when the happy winds were ruffling the waves into sparkling foam, and puffing through the open ward window, the doctor told Aisha he was going to take her home that afternoon in his car.

She lay quietly thinking about it after he had gone. She couldn't be quite sure if she was pleased or not. It was not that she was saying goodbye altogether, because she was coming back to Sunday school every week and bringing Safea with her to visit all the nurses; but six weeks is a long time in the life of a little girl and she had become used to order, cleanliness and space, and all these things were entirely lacking in the shack up the mountain. She thought of the goat, the babies, the cats, the overturned buckets of water, the charcoal smoke, the leaking roof on wet days and the washing that wouldn't dry, and she sighed a little. When the nurse asked her if she wasn't excited, she didn't answer.

The doctor arrived directly after dinner and hustled her off with the voices of the patients ringing in her ears. 'Visit us again, Aisha – go in peace and may God bring you to happiness!' She was unencumbered by any luggage and waved to them with both hands as the car sped out of the gate. Then they were roaring up the mountain road, and the sea through the dip in the hills was far below them and the town far behind them.

The doctor, who had visits further up the mountain, set her down on the slope below her home and bade her goodbye, and for a few moments she stood there alone looking about her. The narcissi were out along the stream bed and black baby lambs gambolled among stretches of blue wild iris. The wind came sweeping up from the sea and, as though it had carried the whisper of her home-coming in its wings, the children suddenly saw her and came tumbling out of the cottage to meet her.

The next few minutes were just a bewildering jumble of shouts and laughter and hugs and kisses, but somehow she

found herself sitting on the cottage steps with the baby on her lap, Absalom behind her with arms clasped tightly round her neck, Mustapha and Sodea, one under each arm, beaming up at her; the goat butted her rather painfully in the back, her mother made mint tea in honour of her home-coming, and Safea stood in front of her on one leg, her slim little body swaying like the mimosa tree in the wind in her ecstasy of joy.

And Aisha, flushed and gloriously happy, suddenly laughed out loud as she remembered the quiet, clean hospital ward and her lovely white bed. She wondered how she had borne living for six weeks away from the hot tight little arms, and the grubby sticky hands of the little brothers and sisters. She looked down at the thin baby with its spotty head and running nose and decided there had never been another child equal to it for beauty and dearness. Her heart was almost bursting with a new awareness of love for them all, and she suddenly remembered and understood why.

She had come to know the other Baby – he was living in her heart, the fountain of all love and gentleness and joy. He was there beside her, shedding his light over the spring hillside, the cottage, the mother and the grimy happy faces of the children, and she saw everything in its blessed glow.

The Heavenly Babe himself had lit the candles.